XOXO

For Pedro, the donkey

©2014 Cameron + Company
6 Petaluma Blvd. North, Suite B6
Petaluma, CA 94952
www.cameronbooks.com

Photographs ©2014 Stephanie Rausser, www.stephanierausser.com
Doll by Jess Brown™, www.jessbrowndesign.com
Text ©2014 Nina Gruener
Edited by Amy Novesky, www.amynovesky.com
Book design by Sara Gillingham Studio, www.saragillingham.com

Library of Congress Control Number: 2013956289
ISBN: 978-1-937359-60-7

Printed in China

We wish to thank the following for all of their contributions to this book:
Kiersten and Joanne Crowley, Conor McCullaugh, Gordon Rausser,
Paige Rausser, Don Frazer, Lawrence Cowell, Lizzie Lehn, Deborah Dapolito,
Pat Sanborn, Suzy Morvay, Kristina Davis, Paige Thomas, Michelle Dotter,
Iain R. Morris, Wovenplay, Flora and Henri, Albert Lamorisse and Pippi.

Photographs by Stephanie Rausser,
Doll by Jess Brown, Story by Nina Gruener

Pip belongs to a girl named Lulu. They live in a
very big city. Wherever Lulu goes, Pip tags along.

Dangling from her girl's arms, Pip's skinny little legs
soar all over town. Lulu knows her way around.

Blue sky plays peekaboo from behind the tall buildings. But the people are too busy to notice.

Lulu is busy, too.

Today they are leaving the city to go on a campout.
Lulu has never been camping before. She has never
slept in a tent or roasted a marshmallow. Mom says
most of her toys won't even work in the country.

But Pip can come along, of course.

They cross the bright orange bridge.
The cold fog whips through their hair.
Lulu squeezes Pip. They are happy
to have each other.

The air turns warm and dusty the farther away from the city they get.

Finally they arrive. An old donkey greets them. Lulu inspects him from afar. He smells funny. Pip thinks he is sweet.

It is a long, slow hike to the campsite.
Lulu and Pip may have overdressed.

And they might have overpacked.

Eventually they reach the river and
make camp. Lulu takes her time to
get everything just right.

There, that's better.

By now the sun is low in the sky and Lulu's tummy growls.

"Time to find a stick," calls Mom.

Lulu and Pip giggle to themselves. Sticks for dinner? They hunt for just the right one. But when Lulu hears something rustle in the bushes, they hurry back to camp.

The campfire pops and hisses. Lulu has never had a hot dog that wasn't from a hot dog stand. It is delicious. Dessert is even better. Shadows dance across their sticky faces.

Lulu thinks about home and wonders if the city lights have come on yet.

Pip looks up at the stars as they start to twinkle, one by one at first, and then a whole sea of them.

They have never seen stars like this before.

Their tent is cozy, but they can't sleep.
First it's too quiet. Then it's too loud.

The wind in the trees.
An orchestra of crickets.
Toads croaking.

And a lonely owl asking
WHO the new girls are.

Eventually they drift off.

Bright sun streams through the tent. Hot chocolate welcomes them. Lulu sips hers quietly. What are they going to do here all day?

After breakfast chores, they head down to the river. It's time to get their feet wet.

Dragonflies and bright green toads dart about as Lulu and Pip begin to explore.

They dig for worms.

Then reel in a rainbow fish as big as Pip!

They splash and play and let
the current take them away.

Then dry in the
warm mountain sun.

They wander in the tall grass, and spot a pair of butterflies. Together they chase them over a hill . . .

. . . and up a tree. Pip had no idea
Lulu could climb a tree. Neither did Lulu.

When the butterflies
disappear high into the
sky, Lulu and Pip flop down
beneath a giant oak tree.

Lulu has new freckles and Pip is nice and dirty.
But as they stare up at the bright blue sky,
there is nowhere else they'd rather be.

Suddenly, the shrub next to them starts to rustle. Lulu looks all around and realizes just how far they've wandered from camp. There are no street signs, no gadgets to consult, not even a trail to follow.

Lulu and Pip are lost.

The shrub rustles again. Pip can feel her girl's heart racing.

Hee-haw.

Lulu has never been so glad to see the donkey! He is pretty sweet.

It's good to have a friend who knows his way around.

Back at camp, Lulu
and Pip insist he join
them for a snack.

That night, after a delicious dinner of rainbow trout, Lulu and Pip collapse into bed.

They wave to the tree branch swaying above, shout "Bravo!" to the crickets and blow kisses to the toads.

Last but not least, they whisper goodnight to the donkey, happily standing by.

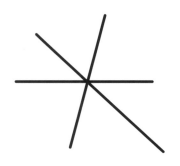

Under a blanket of stars, the doll and her
girl fall fast asleep in the great outdoors.